S0-APO-710

This book belongs to:

____

Enjoy!
Hazel Brink

the Runaway Little Red Lawn Mower

written by **Hazel Brink**

illustrated by **Daren LaVoi**

Expert Publishing, Inc.
Andover, Minnesota

ISBN 10: 1-931945-46-2
ISBN 13: 978-1-931945-46-2

Library of Congress Catalog Number: 2005933985

Printed in South Korea

First Printing: October 2005

08 07 06 05 6 5 4 3 2 1

Expert Publishing, Inc.
14314 Thrush Street NW
Andover, MN 55304-3330
1-877-755-4966
www.expertpublishinginc.com

I dedicate this book to my daughters, Yulah and Loya; foster sons, Martin and Jerry; six grandsons—Gary, Paul, Gregg, Daren, Lauren, Dana; ten great grandchildren—Alison, Adam, Michael, Jenna, Dylan, Haley, Daniel, Josie, Ryan, Luke, and my foster grandchildren.

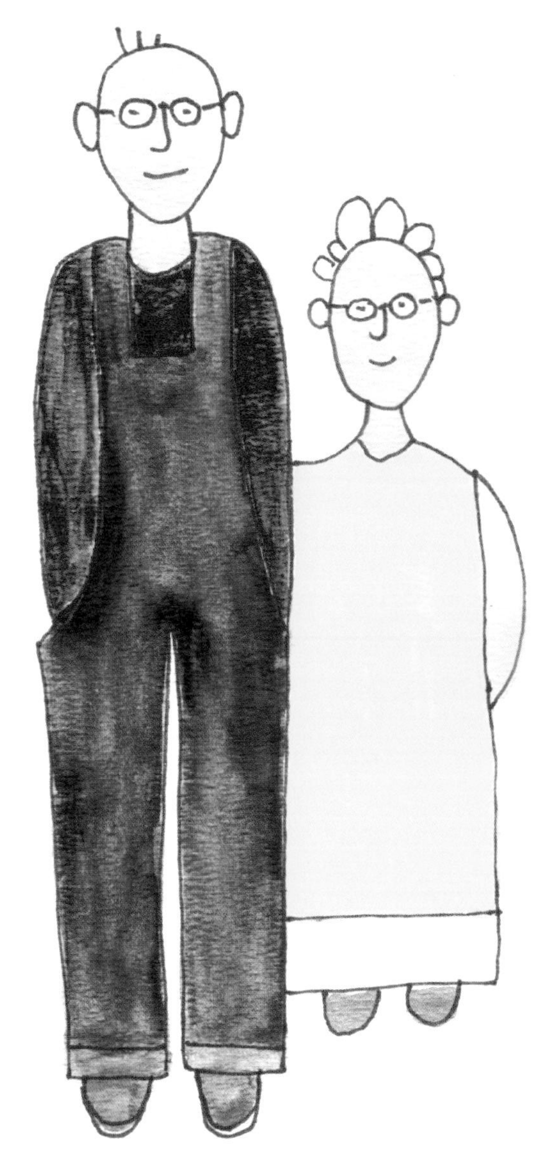

Once upon a time, there was a Great Grandpa and a Great Grandma who lived

in a big gold house
on a hill with lots
of flowers and lots
of grass to mow.

It took Great Grandpa a long time to mow the grass,
and he would get very tired.

One day Great Grandma said, "I will help mow the lawn. I can ride the Little Red Lawn Mower."

"Would you do that, Great Grandma? That would make me very, very happy," responded Great Grandpa.

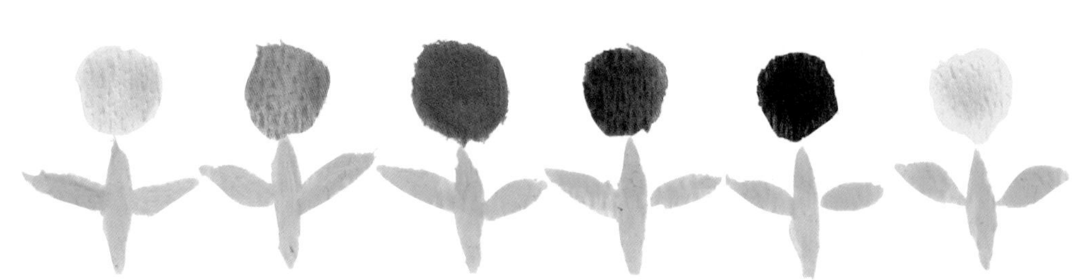

“Yes,” replied Great Grandma.
“That way we can get done faster,
and then maybe we can go and get
a yummy ice cream cone.”

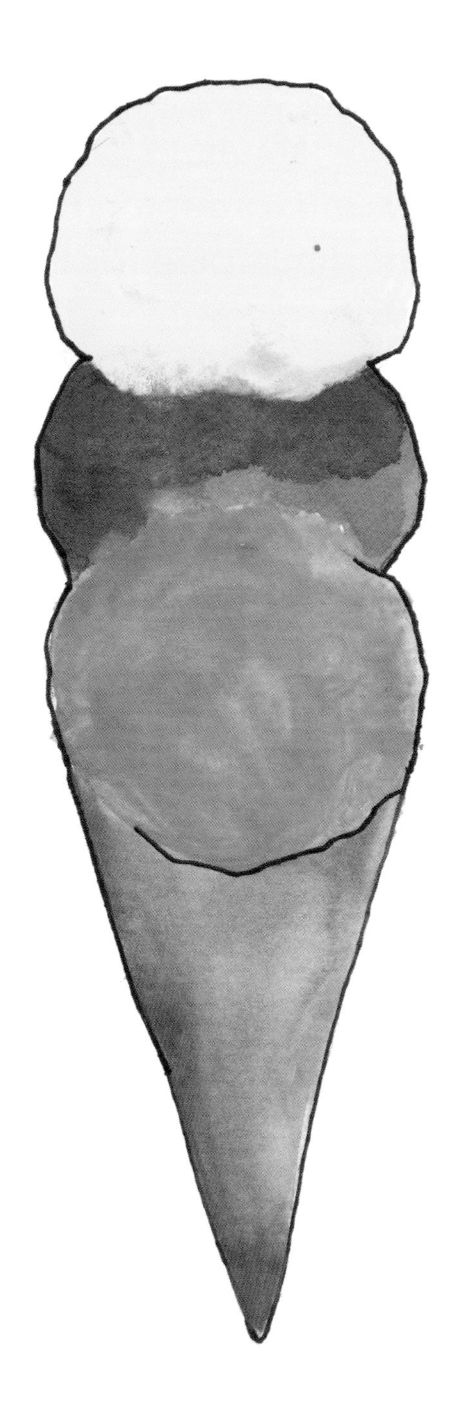

So Great Grandpa hurriedly started the Little Red Lawn Mower and backed it out of the garage for Great Grandma to ride. Great Grandma didn't know much about running a lawn mower, but she knew how to guide it so it could cut the grass.

"Okay," said Great Grandpa, "here it is, all ready for you, but be careful and don't mow down the little trees or flowers."

Great Grandma quickly got on the Little Red Lawn Mower and away she went happily around and around the yard mowing the grass. It was so much fun!

Everything was going just fine, when suddenly Great Grandma felt something on her head. “Oh dear!” said Great Grandma, “That was a raindrop. I will get my hair all wet.”

She had just been to the beauty shop and had her hair fixed so pretty.

Great Grandma quickly jumped off the Little Red Lawn Mower, ran fast into the house, and put on her rain bonnet. Then she quickly dashed out again, and what a surprise! “Where is my Little Red Lawn Mower?” asked Great Grandma. “I left it here. I wonder where it can be?”

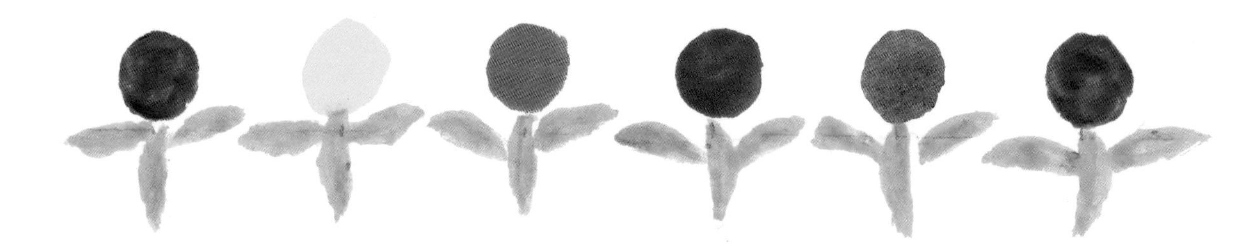

She looked around and saw it was running across the driveway, between the trees, and past a big, big rock.

"You didn't hit me," laughed the Big Rock.

Faster and faster the Little Red Lawn Mower went across the road toward the neighbor's car. "Don't hit me," screamed the Big Gray Car. "I don't want to get all banged up and smashed."

“No, I won’t hurt you. I’m just having fun running away,”
said the Little Red Lawn Mower, mowing all the way.

“ Please stop,” shouted Great Grandma as she ran and tried to catch the Little Red Lawn Mower. But it went faster and faster.

"Stop, please stop!" screamed Great Grandma again, but the Little Red Lawn Mower just wouldn't listen. It kept going faster and faster. It went right by a little evergreen tree.

"Oh, please, Little Red Lawn Mower, don't cut me down. I want to grow tall and be a big Christmas tree some day."

"No, I won't cut you down, Little Evergreen Tree," said the Little Red Lawn Mower.

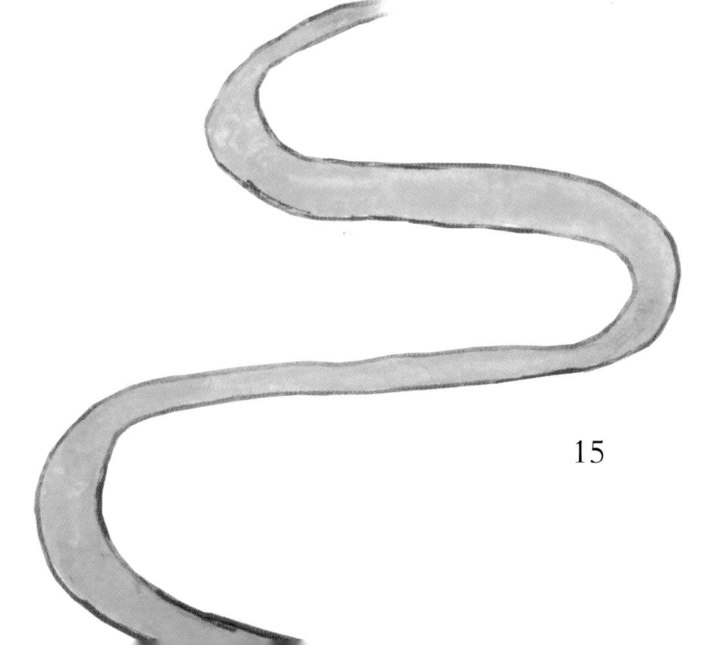

Great Grandma kept running and running until she was out of breath, but the Little Red Lawn Mower went faster than ever.

“Oh, dear,” hollered Great Grandma. “If you don’t stop you will run into the great big lake and drown.” Great Grandma knew that the Little Red Lawn Mower was meant to mow grass and didn’t know how to swim.

But the Little Red Lawn Mower paid no attention.

It just kept going faster and faster and faster. Finally it ran into a big tree and could not go any farther. "You naughty Little Red Lawn Mower," shouted the Big Tree. "I made you stop!"

"Didn't you hear Great Grandma screaming at you to Stop! Stop! Don't you know you are supposed to mind?"

"Thank you, thank you, Big Tree," said Great Grandma. "Thank you for helping me. Now, I must hurry home to tell Great Grandpa what happened."

As Great Grandma rushed home, all the neighbors came out to see what was going on. There was Great Grandpa looking for Great Grandma and the Little Red Lawn Mower. When he saw Great Grandma he asked, “Where have you been? Where is your lawn mower?”

"It's over in the neighbor's yard," answered Great Grandma.

"Over at the neighbor's!" exclaimed Great Grandpa. "What is it doing over there?"

"I went to get my rain bonnet and the Little Red Lawn Mower ran away. I couldn't stop it. It ran across the road, over to the neighbor's, and it wouldn't come home with me," replied Great Grandma.

Great Grandpa felt sorry for Great Grandma.
He patted her on the shoulder and said,
“That’s okay. I’ll go and get the naughty
runaway Little Red Lawn Mower.”

"But remember, Great Grandma, the next time you run into the house to get your rain bonnet, be sure and stop the engine. That Little Red Lawn Mower likes to run away."

After that, whenever Great Grandma helped mow the grass she remembered what Great Grandpa said and stopped the engine when she got off the lawn mower. The Little Red Lawn Mower never ran away again.

The End

About the Author

Hazel A. Brink is a wife, mother, grandmother, music teacher, 4-H leader, oil painter, volunteer, and author.

Whenever a special incident happened involving Grandma and Grandpa, I created a story to make it interesting for the grandkids to read. My daughters encouraged me to publish these stories, so at age 95 I decided to publish *The Runaway Little Red Lawn Mower* as my first book. My teaching career started in South Dakota and Illinois. In 1945, we moved to Minnesota and settled on our own dairy farm in Cohasset. At that time I accepted a position with District 318 as music supervisor of the rural schools, a position I held for thirty years and thoroughly enjoyed. I loved working with children and found each day a new experience. My grandson Daren, an art major, did the illustrations for my book. If God grants me five more years I will have lived a century and seen many changes. Life has many opportunities and one has only to pursue them.

About the Illustrator

The artist, Daren LaVoi, currently resides in south Minneapolis where he maintains a painting studio. His education includes a Bachelor of Arts from Gustavus Adolphus and study at major museums of Europe and the United States. Daren's specialty is oil painting in a contemporary folk art style. He is the grandson of the author, Hazel Brink. Daren, as well as the other grandsons, learned how to mow grass on the Little Red Lawn Mower.